AND ALL THROUGH

THE HOUSE

THE 87TH PRECINCT NOVELS

Cop Hater • The Mugger • The Pusher (1956) The
Con Man • Killer's Choice (1957) Killer's Payoff
• Killer's Wedge • Lady Killer (1958) 'Til Death
• King's Ransom (1959) Give the Boys a Great Big
Hand • The Heckler • See Them Die (1960) Lady,
Lady, I Did It! (1961) The Empty Hours • Like
Love (1962) Ten Plus One (1963) Ax (1964) He
Who Hesitates • Doll (1965) Eight Million Eyes
(1966) Fuzz (1968) Shotgun (1969) Jigsaw (1970)
Hail, Hail, the Gang's All Here (1971) Sadie When
She Died • Let's Hear It for the Deaf Man
(1972) Hail to the Chief (1973) Bread (1974) Blood
Relatives (1975) So Long as You Both Shall Live
(1976) Long Time No See (1977) Calypso (1979)
Ghosts (1980) Heat (1981) Ice (1983) Lightning
(1984) Eight Black Horses (1985) Poison • Tricks
(1987) Lullaby (1989) Vespers (1990) Widows
(1991) Kiss (1992) Mischief (1993)

AND ALL THROUGH ~ THE HOUSE ~

ED McBAIN

ILLUSTRATED BY VICTOR JUHASZ

WARNER BOOKS
A Time Warner Company

Warner Books, Inc., 1271 Avenue of the Americas,
New York, NY 10020
A Time Warner Company

Printed in the United States of America
First Warner Books Printing: November 1994
10 9 8 7 6 5 4 3 2 1

Library of Congress Cataloging-in-Publication Data
McBain, Ed, 1926-
    And all through the house / Ed McBain
      p. cm.
    ISBN 0-446-51845-X
    I. Title
    PS3515.U585A83 1994
    813'.54—dc20   94-20143
                                CIP

Book design by Julia Kushnirsky
Book illustrations by Victor Juhasz

This is for my grandchildren —
Dean and Susan Hunter-Cutrona

Detective Steve Carella was alone in the squad room. It was very quiet for a Christmas Eve.

Normally, all hell broke loose the moment the stores closed. But tonight the squad room and the entire station house seemed unusually still. No phones ringing. No typewriters clacking away. No patrolmen popping upstairs to ask if any coffee was brewing in the clerical office down the hall. Just Carella, sitting at his desk and rereading the D.D. report he'd just typed, checking it for errors. He'd misspelled the "armed" in "armed robbery." It had come out "aimed robbery." He overscored the I with the ballpoint pen, giving the felony its true title. Armed robbery. Little liquor store on Culver Avenue. Guy walked in with a .357 Magnum and an empty potato sack. The owner hit a silent alarm and the two uniforms riding Boy One apprehended the thief as he was leaving the store.

Carella separated the carbons and the triplicate pages—white one in the uppermost basket, pink one in the basket marked for Miscolo in clerical, yellow one for the lieutenant. He looked up at the clock. Ten-thirty. The graveyard shift would be relieving at a quarter to twelve, maybe a bit earlier, since it was Christmas Eve.

God, it was quiet around here.

He got up from his desk and walked around the bank of high cabinets that partitioned the rest of the squad room from a small sink in the corner opposite the detention cage. Quiet night like this one, you could fall asleep on the job. He opened the faucet, filled his cupped hands with water and splashed it onto his face. He was a tall man and the mirror over the sink was set just a little too low to accommodate his height. The top of his head was missing. The mirror caught him just at his eyes, a shade darker than his brown hair and slanted slightly downward to give him a faintly Oriental appearance. He dried his face and hands with a paper towel, tossed the towel into the wastebasket under the sink and then yawned and looked at the clock again, unsurprised to discover that only two minutes had passed since

3

the last time he'd looked at it. The silent nights got to you. He much preferred it when things were really jumping.

He walked to the windows at the far side of the squad room and looked down at the street. Things looked as quiet down there as they were up here. Not many cars moving, hardly a pedestrian in sight. Well, sure, they were all home already, putting the finishing touches on their Christmas trees. The forecasters had promised snow, but so far there wasn't so much as a flurry in the air. He was turning from the window when all of a sudden everything got bloody.

The first thing he saw was the blood streaming down the side of Cotton Hawes's face. Hawes was shoving two white men through the gate in the slatted rail divider that separated the squad room from the corridor outside. The men were cuffed at the wrist with a single pair of cuffs, right wrist to left wrist, and one of them was complaining that Hawes had made the cuff too tight.

"I'll give you tight," Hawes said and shoved again at both men. One of them went sprawling almost headlong into the squad room, dragging the other one with him.

They were both considerably smaller than Hawes, who towered over them like a redheaded fury, his anger somehow pictorially exaggerated by the streak of white in the hair over his right temple, where a burglar had cut him and the hair had grown back white. The white was streaked with blood now from an open cut on his forehead. The cut streamed blood down the right side of his face. It seemed not to console Hawes at all that the two men with him were also bleeding.

"What the hell happened?" Carella asked.

6

He was already coming across the squad room as if someone had called in an assist officer, even though Hawes seemed to have the situation well in hand and this was, after all, a police station and not the big, bad streets outside. The two men Hawes had brought in were looking over the place as if deciding whether or not this was really where they wanted to spend Christmas Eve. The empty detention cage in the corner of the room did not look too terribly inviting to them. One of them kept glancing over his shoulder to see if Hawes was about to shove them again. Hawes looked as if he might throttle both of them at any moment.

"Sit down!" he yelled and then went to the mirror over the sink and looked at his face. He tore a paper towel loose from the holder, wet it and dabbed at the open cut on his forehead. The cut kept bleeding.

"I'd better phone for a meat wagon," Carella said.

"No, I don't need one," Hawes said.

"We need one," one of the two men said.

He was bleeding from a cut on his left cheek. The man handcuffed to him was bleeding from a cut just below his jawline. His shirt was stained with blood, too, where it was slashed open over his rib cage.

Hawes turned suddenly from the sink. "What'd I do with that bag?" he said to Carella. "You see me come in here with a bag?"

"No," Carella said. "What happened?"

"I must've left it downstairs at the desk," Hawes said and went immediately to the phone. He picked up the receiver, dialed three numbers and then said, "Dave, this is Cotton. Did I leave a shopping bag down there at the desk?" He listened and then said, "Would you send one of the blues up with it, please? Thanks a lot." He put the receiver back in

7

the cradle. "Trouble I went through to make this bust," he said, "I don't want to lose the goddamn evidence."

"You ain't got no evidence," the man bleeding from the cheek said.

"I thought I told you to shut up," Hawes said, going to him. "What's your name?"

"I'm supposed to shut up, how can I give you my name?" the man said.

"How would you like to give me your name through a mouthful of broken teeth?" Hawes said. Carella had never seen him this angry. The blood kept pouring down his cheek, as if in visible support of his anger. "What's your goddamn name?" he shouted.

"I'm calling an ambulance," Carella said.

"Good," the man bleeding from under his jawline said.

"Who wants this?" a uniformed cop at the railing said.

"Bring it in here and put it on my desk," Hawes said. "What's your name?"

"Henry," the cop at the railing said.

"Not you," Hawes said.

"Which desk is yours?" the cop asked.

8

"Over there," Hawes said and gestured vaguely.

"What happened up here?" the cop asked, carrying the shopping bag in and putting it on the desk he assumed Hawes had indicated. The shopping bag was from one of the city's larger department stores. A green wreath and a red bow were printed on it. Carella, already on the phone, glanced at the shopping bag as he dialed Mercy General.

"Your name," Hawes said to the man bleeding from the cheek.

"I don't tell you nothing till you read me my rights," the man said.

"My name is Jimmy," the other man said.

"Jimmy what?"

"You dope, don't tell him nothin' till he reads you Miranda."

"You shut up," Hawes said. "Jimmy what?"

"Knowles. James Nelson Knowles."

"Now you done it," the man bleeding from the cheek said.

"It don't mean nothin' he's got my name," Knowles said.

"You gonna be anonymous all night?" Hawes said to the other man.

Into the phone, Carella said, "I'm telling you we've got three people bleeding up here."

"I don't need an ambulance," Hawes said.

"Well, make it as fast as you can, will you?" Carella said and hung up. "They're backed up till Easter, be a while before they can get here. Where's that first-aid kit?" he said and went to the filing cabinets. "Don't we have a first-aid kit up here?"

"This cut gets infected," the anonymous man said, "I'm gonna sue the city. I die in a police station, there's gonna be hell to pay. You better believe it."

"What name should we put on the death certificate?" Hawes asked.

"Who the hell filed this in the missing-persons drawer?" Carella said.

"Tell him your name already, willya?" Knowles said.

"Thomas Carmody, okay?" the other man said. He said it to Knowles, as if he would not allow himself the indignity of discussing it with a cop.

Carella handed the kit to Hawes. "Put a bandage on that, willya?" he said. "You look like hell."

"How about the *citizens?*" Carmody said. "You

see that?" he said to Knowles. "They always take care of their own first."

"On your feet," Carella said.

"Here comes the rubber hose," Carmody said.

Hawes carried the first-aid kit to the mirror. Carella led Carmody and Knowles to the detention cage. He threw back both bolts on the door, took the cuffs off them and said, "Inside, boys." Carmody and Knowles went into the cage. Carella double-bolted the door again. Both men looked around the cage as if deciding whether or not the accommodations suited their taste. There were bars on the cage and protective steel mesh. There was no place to sit inside the cage. The two men walked around it, checking out the graffiti scribbled on the walls. Carella went to where Hawes was dabbing at his cut with a swab of cotton.

"Better put some peroxide on that," he said. "What happened?"

"Where's that shopping bag?" Hawes asked.

"On the desk there. What happened?"

"I was checking out a ten-twenty on Culver and Twelfth, guy went in and stole a television set this guy had wrapped up in his closet, he was giving it to his wife for Christmas, you know? They were next door with their friends, having a drink, burglar must've got in through the fire escape window; anyway, the TV's gone. So I take down all the information—fat chance of ever getting it back—and then I go downstairs, and I'm heading for the car when there's this yelling and screaming up the street, so I go see what's the matter, and these two jerks are arguing over the shopping bag there on the desk."

"It was all your fault," Carmody said to Knowles.

"You're the one started it," Knowles said.

"Anyway, it ain't our shopping bag," Carmody said.

"I figure it's just two guys had too much to drink," Hawes said, putting a patch over the cut, "so I go over to tell them to cool it, go home and sleep it off, this is Christmas Eve, right? All of a sudden, there's a knife on the scene. One of them's got a knife in his hand."

"Not me," Carmody said from the detention cage.

"Not me, either," Knowles said.

"I don't know who started cutting who first," Hawes said, "but I'm looking at a lot of blood.

13

Then the other guy gets hold of the knife some way, and *he* starts swinging away with it, and next thing I know, I'm in the middle of it, and *I'm* cut, too. What it turns out to be—"

"What knife?" Carmody said. "He's dreaming."

"Yeah, what knife?" Knowles said.

"The knife you threw down the sewer on the corner of Culver and Eleventh," Hawes said, "which the blues are out searching in the muck for right this minute. I need this on Christmas Eve," he said, studying the adhesive patch on his forehead. "I really need it."

Carella went to the detention cage, unbolted the door and handed the first-aid kit to Carmody. "Here," he said. "Use it."

"I'm waiting for the ambulance to come," Carmody said. "I want real medical treatment."

"Suit yourself," Carella said. "How about you?"

"If he wants to wait for the ambulance, then I want to wait for the ambulance, too," Knowles said.

Carella bolted the cage again and went back to where Hawes was wiping blood from his hair with a wet towel. "What were they arguing about?" he asked.

"Nobody was arguing," Carmody said.

"We're good friends," Knowles said.

"The stuff in the bag there," Hawes said.

"I never saw that bag in my life," Carmody said.

"Me, either," Knowles said.

"What's in the bag?" Carella asked.

"What do you think?" Hawes said.

"Frankincense," Carmody said.

"Myrrh," Knowles said, and both men burst out laughing.

"My ass," Hawes said. "There's enough pot in that bag to keep the whole city happy through New Year's Day."

"Okay, let's go," a voice said from the railing.

Both detectives turned to see Meyer Meyer lead a kid through the gate in the railing. The kid looked about fourteen years old, and he had a sheep on a leash. The sheep's wool was dirty and matted. The kid looked equally dirty and matted. Meyer, wearing a heavy overcoat and no hat, looked pristinely bald and sartorial by contrast.

"I got us a shepherd," he said. His blue eyes were twinkling; his cheeks were ruddy from the cold outside. "Beginning to snow out there," he said.

"I ain't no shepherd," the kid said.

"No, what you are is a thief, is what you are," Meyer said, taking off his overcoat and hanging it on the rack to the left of the railing. "Sit down over there. Give your sheep a seat, too."

"Sheeps carry all kinds of diseases," Carmody said from the detention cage.

"Who asked you?" Meyer said.

"I catch some kind of disease from that animal, I'll sue the city," Carmody said.

In response, the sheep shit on the floor.

"Terrific," Meyer said. "Whyn't you steal something clean, like a snake, you dummy?"

"My sister wanted a sheep for Christmas," the kid said.

"Steals a goddamn sheep from the farm in the zoo, can you believe it?" Meyer said. "You know

16

what you can get for stealing a sheep? They can send you to jail for twenty years, you steal a sheep."

"*Fifty* years," Hawes said.

"My sister wanted a sheep," the kid said and shrugged.

"His sister is Little Bo-peep," Meyer said. "What happened to your head?"

"I ran into a big-time dope operation," Hawes said.

"That ain't our dope in that bag there," Carmody said.

"That ain't even our bag there," Knowles said.

"When do we get a lawyer here?" Carmody said.

"Shut up," Hawes said.

"Don't tell them nothin' till they read you your rights, kid," Carmody said.

"Who's gonna clean up this sheep dip on the floor?" Carella asked.

"Anybody want coffee?" Miscolo said from outside the railing. "I got a fresh pot brewing in the office." He was wearing a blue sweater over regulation blue trousers, and there was a smile on his face until he saw the sheep. His eyes opened wide. "What's that?" he asked. "A deer?"

17

"It's Rudolph," Carmody said from the detention cage.

"No kidding, is that a *deer* in here?" Miscolo asked.

"It's a raccoon," Knowles said.

"It's my sister's Christmas present," the kid said.

"I'm pretty sure that's against regulations, a deer up here in the squad room," Miscolo said. "Who wants coffee?"

"I wouldn't mind a cup," Carmody said.

"I'd advise against it," Meyer said.

18

"Even on Christmas Eve, I have to take crap about my coffee," Miscolo said, shaking his head. "You want some, it's down the hall."

"I already told you I want some," Carmody said.

"You ain't in jail yet," Miscolo said. "This ain't a free soup kitchen."

"Christmas Eve," Carmody said, "he won't give us a cup of coffee."

"You better get that animal out of here," Miscolo said to no one and went off down the corridor.

"Why won't you let me take the sheep to my sister?" the kid asked.

"'Cause it ain't your sheep," Meyer said. "It

belongs to the zoo. You stole it from the zoo."

"The zoo belongs to everybody in this city," the kid said.

"Tell 'im," Carmody said.

"What's this I hear?" Bert Kling said from the railing. "Inside, mister." His blond

hair was wet with snow. He was carrying a huge valise in one hand, and his free hand was on the shoulder of a tall black man whose wrists were handcuffed behind his back. The black man was wearing a red plaid Mackinaw, its shoulders wet. Snowflakes still glistened in his curly black hair. Kling looked at the sheep. "Miscolo told me it was a deer," he said.

"Miscolo's a city boy," Carella said.

"So am I," Kling said, "but I know a sheep from a deer." He looked down. "Who made on the floor?" he asked.

"The sheep," Meyer said.

"My sister's present," the kid said.

Kling put down the heavy valise and led the black man to the detention cage. "Okay, back away," he said to Carmody and Knowles and waited for them to move away from the door. He unbolted the door, took the cuffs off his prisoner and said, "Make yourself at home." He bolted the door again. "Snowing up a storm out there," he said and went to the coatrack. "Any coffee brewing?"

"In the clerical office," Carella said.

"I meant *real* coffee," Kling said, taking off his

coat and hanging it up.

"What's in the valise?" Hawes asked. "Looks like a steamer trunk you got there."

"Silver and gold," Kling said. "My friend there in the cage ripped off a pawnshop on The Stem. Guy was just about to close, he walks in with a sawed-off shotgun, wants everything in the store. I got a guitar downstairs in the car. You play guitar?" he asked the black man in the cage.

The black man said nothing.

"Enough jewelry in here to make the Queen of England happy," Kling said.

"Where's the shotgun?" Meyer asked.

21

"In the car," Kling said. "I only got two hands." He looked at Hawes. "What happened to your head?" he asked.

"I'm getting tired of telling people what happened to my head," Hawes said.

"When's that ambulance coming?" Carmody asked. "I'm bleeding to death here."

"So use the kit," Carella said.

"And jeopardize my case against the city?" Carmody said. "No way."

Hawes walked to the windows.

"Really coming down out there," he said.

"Think the shift'll have trouble getting in?" Meyer said.

"Maybe. Three inches out there already, looks like."

Hawes turned to look at the clock.

Meyer looked at the clock, too.

All at once, everyone in the squad room was looking at the clock.

The detectives were thinking the heavy snow would delay the graveyard shift and cause them to get home later than they were hoping. The men in the detention cage were thinking the snow might somehow delay the process of criminal justice. The kid sitting at Meyer's desk was thinking it was only half an hour before Christmas and his sister wasn't going to get the sheep she wanted. The squad room was almost as silent as when Carella had been alone in it.

And then Andy Parker arrived with his prisoners.

"Move it," he said and opened the gate in the railing.

Parker was wearing a leather jacket that made him look like a biker. Under the jacket, he was wearing a plaid woolen shirt and a red muffler. The blue woolen watch cap on his head was covered with snow. Even the three-day beard stubble on his face had snowflakes clinging to it. His prisoners

looked equally white, their faces pale and frightened.

The young man was wearing a rumpled black suit, sprinkled with snow that was rapidly melting as he stood uncertainly in the opening to the squad room. Under the suit, he wore only a shirt open at the collar, no tie. Carella guessed he was twenty years old. The young woman with him—*girl,* more accurately—couldn't have been older than sixteen. She was wearing a lightweight spring coat open over what Carella's mother used to call a house dress, a printed cotton thing with buttons at the throat. Her long black hair was dusted with snow. Her brown eyes were wide in her face. She stood shivering just inside the railing, looking more terrified than any human being Carella had ever seen.

She also looked enormously pregnant.

As Carella watched her, she suddenly clutched her belly and grimaced in pain. He realized all at once that she was already in labor.

"I said *move* it," Parker said, and it seemed to Carella that he actually would *push* the pregnant girl into the squad room. Instead, he shoved past the couple and went directly to the coatrack. "Sit down

24

over there," he said, taking off his jacket and hat. "What the hell is that, a sheep?"

"That's my sister's Christmas present," the kid said, though Parker hadn't been addressing him.

"Lucky her," Parker said.

There was only one chair alongside his desk. The young man in the soggy black suit held it out for the girl, and she sat in it. He stood alongside her as Parker took a seat behind the desk and rolled a sheaf of D.D. forms into the typewriter.

"I hope you all got chains on your cars," he said to no one and then turned to the girl. "What's your name, sister?" he asked.

"Maria Garcia Lopez," the girl said and winced again in pain.

"She's in labor," Carella said and went quickly to the telephone.

"You're a doctor all of a sudden?" Parker said and turned to the girl again. "How old are you, Maria?" he asked.

"Sixteen."

"Where do you live, Maria?"

"Well, thass the pro'lem," the young man said.

"Who's talking to you?" Parker said.

"You were assin' Maria—"

"Listen, you understand English?" Parker said. "When I'm talkin' to this girl here, I don't need no help from—"

"You wann' to know where we live—"

"I want an address for this *girl* here, is what I—"

"You wann' the address where we *s'pose'* to be livin'?" the young man said.

"All right, what's *your* name, wise guy?" Parker said.

"José Lopez."

"The famous bullfighter?" Parker said and turned to look at Carella, hoping for a laugh.

Carella was

on the telephone. Into the receiver, he said, "I *know* I already called you, but now we've got a pregnant woman up here. Can you send that ambulance in a hurry?"

"I ain' no bullfighter," José said to Parker.

"What are you, then?"

"I wass cut sugar cane in Puerto Rico, but now I don' have no job. Thass why my wife an' me we come here this city, to fine a job. Before d' baby comes."

"So what were you doing in that abandoned building?" Parker said and turned to Carella again. "I found them in an abandoned building on South Sixth, huddled around this fire they built."

Carella had just hung up the phone. "Nothing's moving out there," he said. "They don't know *when* the ambulance'll be here."

"You know it's against the law to take up residence in a building owned by the city?" Parker said. "That's called squatting, José, you know what squatting is? You also know it's against the law to set fires inside buildings? That's called arson, José, you know what arson is?"

"We wass cold," José said.

"Ahhh, the poor kids were cold," Parker said.

"Ease off," Carella said softly. "It's Christmas Eve."

"So what? That's supposed to mean you can break the law, it's Christmas Eve?"

"The girl's in labor," Carella said. "She may have the baby any damn minute. Ease off."

Parker stared at him for a moment and then turned back to José. "Okay," he said, "you came up here from Puerto Rico looking for a job—"

"Sí, señor."

"Talk English. And don't interrupt me. You came up here lookin' for a job; you think jobs grow on trees here?"

"My cousin says he hass a job for me. D' factory where he works, he says there's a job there. He says come up."

"Oh, now there's a cousin," Parker said to Hawes, hoping for a more receptive audience than he'd found in Carella. "What's your cousin's name?" he asked José.

"Cirilo Lopez."

"Another bullfighter?" Parker said and winked at Hawes. Hawes did not wink back.

"Whyn't you leave him alone?" Carmody said from the cage.

Parker swiveled his chair around to face the cage. "Who said that?" he asked and looked at the black man. "You the one who said that?"

The black man did not answer.

"I'm the one who said it," Carmody admitted.

"What are you in the cage for?"

"Holding frankincense and myrrh," Carmody said and laughed. Knowles laughed with him. The black man in the cage did not crack a smile.

"How about you?" Parker asked, looking directly at him.

"He's mine," Kling said. "That big valise there is full of hot goods."

"Nice little crowd we get here," Parker said and swiveled his chair back to the desk. "I'm still waitin' for an address from you two," he said. "A *legal* address."

"We wass s'pose' to stay with my cousin," José said. "He says he hass a room for us."

"Where's that?" Parker asked.

"Eleven twenny-four Mason Avenue, apar'men' thirty-two."

"But there's no room for us," Maria said. "Cirilo, he's—" She caught her breath. Her face contorted in pain again.

José took her hand. She looked up at him. "D' lady lives ness door," he said to Parker, "she tells us Cirilo hass move away."

"When's the last time you heard from him?"

"Lass' month."

"So you don't think to check, huh? You come all the way up from Puerto Rico without checkin' to see your cousin's still here or not? Brilliant. You hear this, Bert?" he said to Kling. "Jet-set travelers we got here; they come to the city in their summer clothes in December, they end up in an abandoned building."

"They thought the cousin was still here, that's all," Kling said, watching the girl, whose hands were now spread wide on her belly.

"Okay, what's the big emergency here?" someone said from the railing.

The man standing there was carrying a small black satchel. He was wearing a heavy black overcoat over white trousers and tunic. The snow on the shoulders of the coat and dusted onto his bare head was as white as the tunic and pants. "Mercy General at your service," he said. "Sorry to be so late; it's been a busy night. Not to mention two feet of snow out there. Where's the patient?"

"You'd better take a look at the girl," Carella said, "She's in —"

"Right here," Carmody said from the cage.

"Me, too," Knowles said.

"Somebody want to let them out?" the intern said. "One at a time, please."

Hawes went to the cage and threw back the bolts on the door.

"Who's first?" the intern said.

Carella started to say, "The girl over there is in la—"

"Free at last," Carmody interrupted, coming out of the cage.

"Don't hold your breath," Hawes said and bolted the door again.

32

The intern was passing Parker's desk when Maria suddenly gasped.

"You okay, miss?" he said at once.

Maria clutched her belly.

"Miss?" he said.

Maria gasped again and sucked in a deep breath of air.

Meyer rolled his eyes. He and Miscolo had delivered a baby right here in the squad room not too long ago, and he was grateful for the intern's presence.

"This woman is in *labor!*" the intern said.

"Comes the dawn," Carella said, sighing.

"Iss it d' baby comin'?" José asked.

"Looks that way, mister," the intern said. "Somebody get a blanket or something. You got any blankets up here?"

Kling was already on his way out of the squad room.

"Just take it easy, miss," the intern said. "Everything's gonna be fine." He looked at Meyer and said, "This is my first baby."

Terrific, Meyer thought, but he said nothing.

"You need some hot water?" Hawes asked.

"That's for the movies," the intern said.

"Get some hot water," Carmody said.

"I don't need hot water," the intern said. "I just need someplace for her to lie down." He thought about this for a moment. "Maybe I *do* need hot water," he said.

Hawes ran out of the squad room, almost colliding with Kling, who was on his way back with a pair of blankets he'd found in the clerical office. Miscolo was right behind him.

"Another baby coming?" he asked Meyer. He seemed eager to deliver it.

"We got a professional here," Meyer said.

"You need any help," Miscolo said to the intern, "just ask, okay?"

"I won't need any help," the intern said, somewhat snottily, Miscolo thought. "Put those blankets down someplace. You okay, miss?" He suddenly looked very nervous.

Maria nodded and then gasped again and clutched her belly and stifled a scream. Kling was spreading one of the blankets on the floor to the left of the detention cage, near the hissing radiator. Knowles and the black man moved to the side of the cage nearest the radiator.

"Give her some privacy," Carella said softly. "Over there, Bert. Behind the filing cabinets."

Kling spread the blanket behind the cabinets.

"She's gonna have her baby right here," Knowles said.

The black man said nothing.

"I never experienced nothin' like this in my life," Knowles said, shaking his head.

The black man still said nothing.

"Maria?" José said.

Maria nodded and then screamed.

"Try to keep it down, willya?" Parker said. He looked as nervous as the intern did.

"Just come with me, miss," the intern said, easing Maria out of the chair, taking her elbow and guiding her to where Kling had spread the blanket behind the cabinets. "Easy, now," he said. "Everything's gonna be fine."

Hawes was back with a kettle of hot water. "Where do you want—" he started to say, just as Maria and the intern disappeared from view behind the bank of high cabinets.

It was three minutes to midnight, three minutes to Christmas Day.

From behind the filing cabinets, there came only the sounds of Maria's labored breathing and the intern's gentle assurances that everything was going to be all right. The kid kept staring at the clock as it threw the minutes before Christmas into the room. Behind the filing cabinets, a sixteen-year-old girl and an inexperienced intern struggled to bring a life into the world.

35

There was a sudden sharp cry from behind
the cabinets.

The hands of the clock stood straight up.

It was Christmas Day.

"Is it okay?" Parker asked. There was something like concern in his voice.

"Fine baby boy," the intern said, as if repeating
a line he'd heard in a movie. "Where's that water?
Get me some towels. You've got a fine, healthy boy,
miss," he said to Maria and covered her with the
second blanket.

36

Hawes carried the kettle of hot water to him.

Carella brought him paper towels from
the rack over the sink.

"Just going to wash him off a little, miss," the intern said.

"You got a fine baby boy," Meyer
said to José, smiling.

José nodded.

"What're you gonna name him?"
Kling asked.

The black man, who'd been silent
since he'd entered the squad room, suddenly said in a deep and sonorous voice,

"'Behold, a virgin shall conceive and bear a son, and his name shall be called Emmanuel.'"

"Amen," Knowles said.

The detectives were gathered in a knot around the bank of filing cabinets now, their backs to Carmody. Carmody could have made a run for it, but he didn't. Instead, he picked up first the shopping

bag of marijuana he and Knowles had been busted
for and then the valise containing the loot Kling
had recovered when he'd collared the black man.
He carried them to where Maria lay behind the

cabinets, the baby on her breast. He knelt at her feet. He dipped his hand into the bag, grabbed a handful of pot and sprinkled it onto the blanket. He opened the valise. There were golden rings and silver plates in the valise, bracelets and necklaces, rubies and diamonds and sapphires that glittered in the pale, snow-reflected light that streamed through the corner windows.

"Gracias," Maria said softly. *"Muchas gracias."*

Carella, standing closest to the windows, looked up at the sky, where the snow still swirled furiously.

"That's not a bad name," Meyer said to José. "Emmanuel."

"I will name him Carlos," José said. "After my father."

Carella turned from the windows.

"What'd you expect to see out there?" Parker asked. "A star in the East?"